33 Crystal Skulls & The Anti+Christ

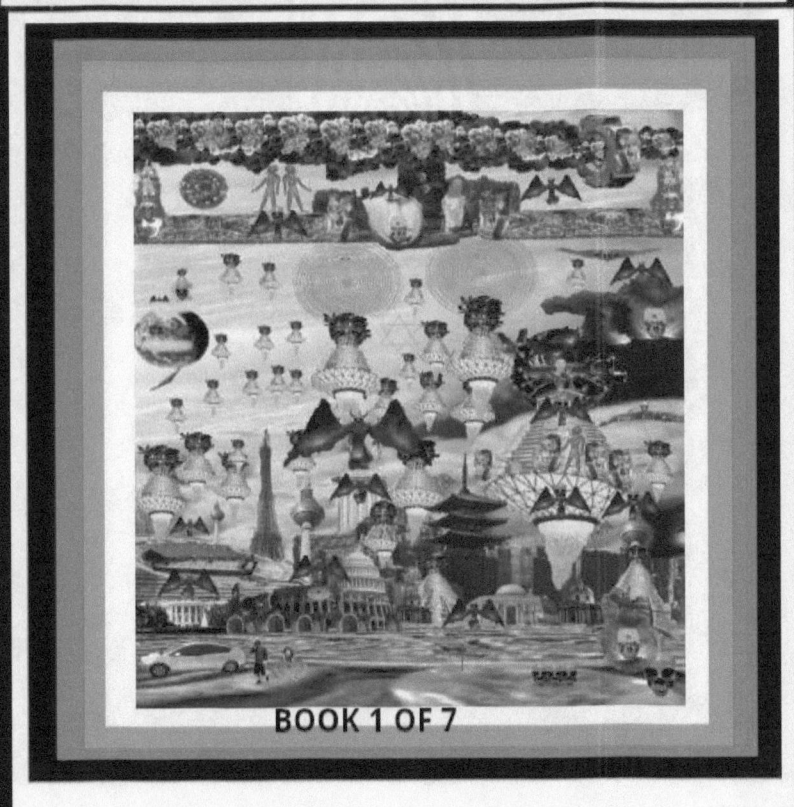

BOOK 1 OF 7

33 Crystal Skulls & The Anti+Christ

UNCENSORED, UNEDITED,
RETRACTED INVENTION VERSION

1ST EDITION MANUSCRIPT

Paperback or Hardcover
I.S.B.N NUMBER   978-1-967897-11-7
33 Crystal Skulls & The Anti+Christ CHAPTER 1 PART 1- 7

Dedicated to

GOD

In God we trust.

Our true spark of, cosmic static, spiral core of all our inner sparks, ghosts / spirits. Whatever the force within us, is called.

God is perpetually awesome.
Thank you God for everything.
Please forgive our iniquities.
1971-266

33 Crystal Skulls & The Anti+Christ

A glimpse of what a strange and mysterious prophesy looks like or just an opinion of what was or will be, after life after death or vise versa.
Why does history repeat itself?

33 Crystal Skulls & The Anti+Christ

UNCENSORED, UNEDITED, RETRACTED INVENTION VERSION

1ST EDITION

The Book by RAPHAEL/ Rafael G.

The Human breath of life. An internal, Autonomous program, for humans, extra sensory boost of pure life. An App/program defibrillator life support, for emergencies, for Humans.

E-BOOK   978-1-967897-01-8
PAPERBACK   978-1-967897-11-7
HARDCOVER

33 Crystal Skulls & The Anti+Christ
Chapter 1, PART 1 OF 7

33 Crystal Skulls & The Anti+Christ

UNCENSORED, UNEDITED, RETRACTED INVENTION VERSION

GOD'S WORDS ARE IN OUR HUMAN CODE

1ST EDITION MANUSCRIPT

by RAPHAEL / Rafael G.

CHAPTER ONE

The Conference

The Conference.

33 Crystal Skulls & their,

Illuminated Chakras 1971.

The inspired Awakening.

33 energized brilliant Zifi,

illuminating, multi changing colored, human

like Crystal Skulls are being preliminarily placed, in existing, and rebuilt pyramidical monuments around the world. These 33 Zifi Crystal Skulls have a tiny flower shaped diamond inside. Rare metals, gold, and crystals were embedded within the Crystal Skulls. Emerged, and preserved, tiny Angelic specs of brain membranes, from our past leaders of the future historical 12 Nations. You could say, a Prius, per say. Ancient Mummies were carried in festivals every year, until their rebirth. The Zifi Crystal Skulls, are each strategically, facing a direction to a specific, marked solar system in the sky. Our inner, human membrane satellite station galactic brain maps, previously installed, turns on. Not just instinct, but a clairvoyant, manner of insertion, by static injection.

28 of the Zifi Crystal Skulls placements are in very highly elevated 24 karat, golden pyramid pillars. They are above, certain exact elevations of, 333-666 feet from the ground up. The Zifi Crystal Skulls are placed on this planet strategically, and are exact elevations from the planets floor foundation, going vertically from the ground up. The elevation has to be exactly, 333-666 feet up from the ground of the planet. Or the awakening will, not awaken. The year is 1971, last week of November.

28 of the Zifi Crystal Skulls are placed in Geo -metrically, precise locations all around, criss-crossed locations, on enormous pyramidical pillars, situated on the planet. The Zifi Crystal Skulls are normal, variety of different human sizes,

except the 33rd purple Zifi Crystal Skull.
The 33rd Zifi Crystal Skull is the largest
of the Zifi Crystal Skulls. It was created
when the planet was molded, and is what it
is, partially today.

The 33rd Crystal Skull, is located
deep inside, the center of the planets
secret destination. It is hidden deep inside
a Crystal Cavern, and golden remote core, of
our planet. The Zifi Crystal Skulls
Latitude, and Longitude placements, will
coincide with each of the Zifi Crystal
Skulls coordinated placements, around the
planet.

The Crystal Skulls are strategically
placed, as similar to the way satellites
measuring G.P.S. coordinates above us, and
are placed around the planet. Each Zifi

Crystal Skull has an inner data stream that is said to be the fastest data stream speed in the galaxy.

(Time, and life continues: The future, present day.)

All the 33 Zifi Crystal Skulls are beginning to be correctly placed, as per the founded instructional data, that was given to the laboring Scientist team from the N.S. CC33 A. (National Secret CC33 Association). The Zifi Crystal Skulls begin to immediately vibrate an ancient humming bird, sound affects, as the correct placements of all the Zifi Crystal Skulls are closely reached.

The humming sound begins when six of the Crystal Skulls are placed in the exact correct sequence, facing the correct

Longitude, and Latitude toward the Northern
Hemisphere, while the other correctly,
sequenced when twenty six face the Southern
Hemisphere.

             The conference, begins.

        As the guest speaker, and live,
testimony from Mic Ki Malokota, will now
continue to explain.)

        "The unity of humanity is now
imminent. As for our diplomatic world order,
have created our 12 nations, and a
functional world system, for humans are now
in protocol for functional progression,
without ceasing. Every branch of the human
life will live in peace. Now.

One secret requirement break through
that was discovered, is that the eyes of the
Skulls needed to be looking, and facing
certain port bound directions to the skies,
precisely, and be in the correct digital
locations, high off the ground of the
planet. Or it will fail.

We now will, take you live to the
convention where the Attorney General, and
the top highest ranked Scientist in their
respected fields of special studies, are
gathered, at this present time. The human
guests, attendees at the summit, are
currently the smartest people on this planet
on record. They will now elaborate. "

As Attorney General, and top
Scientist, Mcduphelknewberi now, begins his
live testimony.

"We, from the International
Scientist Association are allowed to finally
announce, that we have discovered ancient
Zifi Crystal Skulls that will impact
humanity extremely positively, and if
instructions are not respected, perhaps the
outcome will be, negatively.

We discovered these Zifi Crystal
Skulls in many different regions, and have
been able to finally round up, all 33 of
them. Most of the codes have been broken,
and we will coordinate many new technical
break troughs to function, progress, and
improve mankind. We have been extracting
data held within the inner Zifi Crystal
Skulls for decades.

This data that we've been extracting, and up linking with man-made devices of our current times are storing so much data from the Zifi Crystal Skulls, since the early twenties. We've been retrieving data from the Zifi Crystal Skulls to this day, and we are still down loading data from the Zifi Crystal Skulls. As this, may take a few life times to extract all the data.

Scientists discovered in the 40's a projection of a Golden hologram that was projected by the now famous, and infamous Zifi Pink Crystal Skull, we call, (Zifi Pinkiy). Predeceasing Scientists were able to retrieve some of the data from the 1st Zifi Pink Crystal Skull that was discovered buried, in Mexico in The Cholola Pyramid.

Number 5 crystal skull in Rio De Puestonero had the Moons face embedded into the skull,

and a secret location integrated into the skull with a royal blue diamond showing the spot of

the 14th skulls location on the Moon. When the discovery was made, priority became a race

for humans to get to the moon.

Some were hidden on the Moon. As when the discovery took place. We sent a robotic dune buggy machine, which could adapt to the Moon. It communicates data when movement is located.

A real blessing.

The earlier quadruple laser readers that Scientist used in the 30's, pulled out so much data, in those days, they had to use data tape as the storage medium. And that is why computers back then used large rooms that would be filled by large computers. They were, filling up warehouses, just with data tape.

To this day we are still pulling new life visions of mankind, data from the same, Zifi Pink Crystal Skull. We are still downloading, information. But with newer, and advance technology methods. Screens are different but, you could say, the same technology.

We now are using special Crystals cut into Skulls to hold the new data as we too used primitive CDs, Hard drives SD, SSD, micro chips, microfiche, silicone, DVDs, Blue ray, and many other data storage devices, but crystals by far are the best, and have held the most data.

The 33 Crystal Skulls are beyond a normal planet crystal. We are not sure, the difference, why a regular crystal does not match up, to The Crystal Skulls, capacity. Maybe the human brain tissue or software, or even a soul is in these devices. But they are Genuine, and work better.

We our still stumbling on new math codes to be able to expand the crystals capacities from the Zifi Pink Crystal Skull. Technology with algorithm break through, happen every day. We still to this minute are pulling more info every day, from our friendly Zifi Pink Crystal Skull.

This Month we will be lending, Zifi Pinkiy the Crystal Skull to a new mapping experiment that was downloaded 20 years ago. New info had determined it might be beneficial to try this experiment. Thus, far the Zifi Crystal Skulls have advanced, and progressed humanity many folds.

The downloaded data from the Zifi Pink Crystal Skull has advanced all fields even new calculation advancements. A break through without recognition, till they showed up. As, these new developments of mapping of today's brain, and chemistry charts, has surpassed yesterdays science of technology by 10 folds. Area 51 was a smoke screen.

This Months experiment, I am told is an exciting advancement for the planet. I am told, these experiments we will be conducting are similar to 33 supped up on extra boosted, steroids, machine. The Zifi Crystal Skulls, will become, super transmitting, mesmerizing antennas. But, being supped up, on a human crystalline, bio code, transmission levels.

Certain, brain receptors will acknowledge all the signals or what we now call natural brain electronic receptor synapses. The natural human membrane wiring receptors will be induced, and integrate, evolution by the transmitted signal. By the natural, human brain structure, that loops in the internal brain, makes this a possibility. Similar, to coils, connecting through induction. The human hardware was naturally, and chemically instructed to be conceivably pre installed at conception, naturally. The strands of life, or the DNA code are similar, to storage devices. But without a soul. The magic Crystalline blood we carry connects us. The vibrations induce us.

Like a remote control, connects to devices.

Some Scientists say. Brain control has been awakened by this unity of re-creating the ancient hardware our ancestors had intended for today's world. Using Crystalline technology conducting principles. If I didn't see what I saw I would think it is crazy mad & not true. But I now know it is true, from what my own eyes have seen, and the visions I dream at night, make it very clear.

6 positive vibrating, brilliantly sparkling colored Zifi Crystal Skulls are precisely placed on top of very well hidden, 24 karats, golden monumental pyramids. All these monuments are disguised in plain locations, across the world, and in very famous sites.

But the monuments cleverly masked, to appear to be, something different, and hidden, from vandals. The Zifi Crystal Skulls were placed in the prior, 12 nations with special monuments. One popular placement was the popular circle of Ironyland.

(Stone Hedge replications on Planets.)

History of dedicated chemistry has verified that Stone Hedge's carbon stones have concluded that the stones are the exact match of the same material from which was transported to Stone Hedge, 5,000 miles away. By scientific conclusion, and forensic studies, have proved the stones to be exact matches.

Proving both tested stone material was conclusive, and was discovered to be from mountains 15,000 miles away."

The Attorney general takes out a handkerchief, and wipes his perspiring head, and continues.

"In 1943 the Attorney General from the Scientists Association Committee, mandated to precisely create a completed circle at Stone Hedge. Or construct a completed format of what a similar Stone Hedge future energy spot would look like. We will be using the exact stone from the mountains many miles away. We now promise that we will complete, these new projects, but Historical monuments, and cultured projects.

We will retrieve whatever materials needed, as a humanitarian duty to finish this advanced civilized culture of tomorrow. Today. The current schematics we have from Zifi Pinkiy, propose an electronically completed monument configuration, using the planet, like a giant motherboard on a computer. All that would be required for the projects completion of what it might have looked like, are the finished historical

monuments all around the world, be exposed
as a key point.

Then be energetically, plugged in
wireless. Connected with the correct unique
algorithm, to The Zifi Crystal Skulls,
located around the world. There are more
unfinished Monuments in certain parts of the
planet that as a world Galaxy Nation, it is
our obligation-al duty to complete all
historical monuments, and future time pieces
of our current advancing technological world
order. The orders for all the other
historical monuments, is to cut, and
complete an actual computer motherboard, on
this Planet. The motherboard would function
by closing certain circuits around the
world. Sparks would travel around the world,
with humans inside protected oval shell.
Wireless transports as certain Mayan

civilizations, and other connected cultures, that used spark time technologies. And using power from the invisible energy in the air, we exist on. The real grid.

Reconnecting, the world Pyramids, once more, to the octagon web. Fitting the already started circular Stone Hedge monument, as another part of the connecting pieces. The stone lid capacitor would be in the center, holding large electronic resonating cosmetic beams from certain ion beams from Nova flares.

Thus, completing the project. Compiling a closed circuit to the last detail of The Zifi Crystal Skulls, detailed instructions, from the projected futuristic capacitive, schematic diagrams. Even the large Gold Pro tonic, hieroglyphic, Pyramid

conducting pieces, that sit on top of each
monument, is needed for all to function.
Dismissing any trespass laws, allowing all
to use the spark technology, of future
transportation.

They are strategically needed at the
center point located on this planet. The
monuments are easily charged from the simple
Ionic static, created around you, making the
phenomenon function. The public was told, in
1943 that none of the projects have been
completed.

The projects were reported, never
completed as the churches were against the
idea. The church leaders said the Zifi
Crystal Skulls were of Satan's descending
family.

These images of course being very questionable, for two of the Ruby Red, Zifi Crystal Skulls. But we know it being untrue for the other, 31 Zifi Crystal Skulls. As when past Scientist first began to crack the codes, and eventually the correct data streamline illustrated the true details of history.

First instructions were for the same goals. For humanity to unite and finish, all the uncompleted, historic, monumental projects, around the world. On record these tasks were never completed. As that is what the general public was told. Some monuments were replicated, and tourists were led to fake monuments. Known as, Stone Hedge the capacitor, on some planets. Keeping the real Capacitive, finished product away from the human minds eyes. Some humans, being around

the structures, would have seizures around
the lights.

The Goal was to make the planet into
a Mega Mother-ship. Moving the planets
gravitational elements, to galaxies far in
space. This large Motherboard planet is the
main connection, as the ground we walk on,
is the ground. Sun sparks nova flares, like
a synapse fires flares. This large, and
small concepts induce these two together, to
become, the passage of time travel, using
special vehicles. A solar flare is outside
your doors, but you do not see it.

The ancient habit ants knew, and
would use Planets as mother ship worm holes,
for travel through the Universes. Collecting
gold asteroids, lithium, current
commodities, live stocks or other raw

limited materials, from near by asteroids or planets. This key is one of the gifts left behind by our higher powers, allowing unlimited possibilities of travel. This would allow planet jumping transportation possible. Similar to the way arching high voltage lightning strikes, and explodes, during a storm. Saving, your Planets, from imminent, destruction. From the effect, of old Super Novas, imploding.

The other uncompleted land marks needed special material with certain resisting stones that were also strategically placed. All across the world were accommodated, by the mapping schematics, that were generated from the Pink Zifi Crystal Skull.

This world is very powerful, and if used correctly, it is a spaceship / motherboard, With electricity powering a huge Golden computer chip, if the gold, and components are placed, and charged correctly. The big ride of our planet would benefit, controlling the magnetic fluctuating sphere as our main frame vehicle, our planet. Humans have damaged the balance of materials around the world, needing adjustments to make the galaxies not collide with each other, in the future.

Otherwise, as time goes on, and if the world gets UN balanced, by material, moving from one continent, to another continent. The other side of the world, might fluctuate the invisible, and inductive wave we are on. What do you think will happen to an uneven planet? The heavier side starts sinking? Over the same action occurring, more than 1,000 years would definitely cause an unbalanced planet to occur. Fluctuate, a dancing persona repeating over, and over. Would it balance out, or would your planet suck a meteorite, to the uneven ground? Mother nature at work.

Let us, just say, you take out half of the world oil, consistently, more than 300 or 600 years. Then what will happen to the planets balance? Water is not oil. The compounds are different. You cannot combine or replace the oil with water. Different properties, will compress, differently. You cannot put water in an automobile master cylinder instead of brake fluid. Your vehicle will not stop. So do not try it. The water will evaporate causing air in the system, and causing chaos. Heavier islands wash away. The world actions cause the world reactions. Could this be a weapon of war, or the needs of mankind?

Six other darker Zifi Crystal Skull devices were also placed in plain location of historical, monuments. Some on secret Government bases, that was previously discovered to be from pre built, and abandoned Mayan pyramids, or by some advance ancient humans, millions of years ago.

These instructions, and locations were strategically pre mapped by ancient builders for the connection of an advance, and technological working mind control, networks system. The similarities of all the geometrical landmarks, of ancient monuments had the same characteristics of being created by the same clan, on all the same pages at the same time. We did not believe this. However, we have confirmed this to be true, since all the internal towers were created with the same technological principles.

These monuments were replicated to be similar, and to be exact, giant Tesla coils. All, were to be the same. Except the unfinished monuments, which were found wired with ancient ore-existing hypertension Tesla golden coils, were disrupted. All the coils were built within, and hidden inside the towers, monumental guts. If all the ancient geometric circuits were completed, then the monuments would be able to blast a Zifi force field effect around the world. 500G

tiny vibrations. A cloak wove heavily, for
your planet.

    The outcome would be free energy,
and more advanced, amazing flying machines
would now exist. The outcome would be
similar to connecting your cell devices,
tablets, cellular phones, Terra Plate, or
any other device on a cell or wi fi towers.

    But instead of a cell or wi fi
devices, the connections would be bigger
items like auto-flying vehicles, planes,
and anything else that you could imagine,
that you want to float in the air. This is
possible with the correct computer
programming frequency signal receptors
running at the same time across peaceful
nations. To declare, People of God's Planet,
and Justice For All. All Human Lives

Matter. Take the lease back permanently, from the Devil.

A sophisticated harmonious balance of static controlled electrical currents, are being projected, and invisible signals are live streamed across the planet. It is similar to any electrical device that has a motherboard. Metaphorically, and logically speaking, you have the planet which is a huge Motherboard, and everything else on her is the smaller constructed component. Some devices, with large golden components, were the main source, with their own special conductive principles. Some static light beams, being smaller than nanobot technology. Streaming life, to biodegradable cleaning agents, for the planets own, natural immune system.

As the system being so large, you can say mirrors similarly to how, faxes work, on a big scale, and allows transportation in the same manner. The same way a single capillary cleanses the dissolution of carbon dioxide from a human body receptor doing its job, directed by the brain above. Now you put all the connections together, and you will have the worlds most peaceful, war machine in the galaxy.

The power to have the smallest planet in the solar system, and be able to annihilate all the other planets at will if desired. If a completed closed connection to the device was achieved, the system would allow similar functions to be controlled by the brain to do so."

(The Bible has declared: As to have
faith, to believe, as small as a mustard
seed, then we will be able to move
mountains.) As small as a mustard seed, is
nano technology.

"These ancient civilizations,
discovered Tesla buildings are now mostly
hidden, and covered up by military
camouflage, and are very well guarded in
bases around the world.

Some of the Golden buildings have
fake facets of famous land marks that are
dressed up to appear to be something
different, and hidden from the minds eyes.

These incomplete locations were in
plain sites around the world, but were
hidden from the public, by contemporary

masked structures to appear to be something else, for security purposes.

These, famous, land marks, attract repeating tourists, visiting every year, not knowing the true potential, and power that these monuments have held hidden for centuries. Some of the internal 24k golden pillars had to be reconnected back to the golden Tesla coiled pillars, as vandals, and thieves not knowing what they were doing, took parts from them, during time of human wars.

Some of the pillars were not completely connected or finished. As some of the circuits were severed, and an open connection was lost from tampering thieves taking the gold components, that closed the connection, inside the monumental pyramids.

This would render the whole planet motherboard devices useless. Without all the advance golden connections at functional optimization, no human would be able to tap into the correct frequencies of these units. Hence, the monuments would not function correctly, or at all.

The internal golden motherboard circuits, of some of the pillars had been disconnected for centuries, by thieves stealing some of the 24 karats, hieroglyphic prescribed Golden Tablets, and Golden Pyramids. The thieves did not know the Golden Tablets true purpose. The thieves would try to profit from, selling the Golden tablets.

Many of the Golden Tablets secrets were lost by the melting of the gold for sale. All the golden internal pillar monuments have all the same internals working principles, and functions, but with different facets.

As all of the pyramidical units, were mirrored, to be similar, and, have the same functions, for being the homes, of The Zifi Crystal Skulls. Literally a treasure Terra machine.

All the internal hardware, of the pyramids, were copied, internally, to function, as one major component for the planet An Advanced Aerial system control. One main function, is it created an open working united planetarium ionic air wave network system. The pinnacle of networks.

As some of the homes for each of these Zifi Crystal Skulls were ancient monumental buildings, and each had its own facet of different styles externally, but the integrations were all internally the same.

The internal guts of all the monuments had the same instructions from the makers 6D printers, and with the same schematic principles.

The insides were mirrored, and mimicked to be exactly the same internally to make this great amazing network system functional. The process involved giant space crafts or drones, working as wireless printers. The men would assist these mighty machines to precision accomplishments every time.

The ancient builders around the world all had the internal blueprints for hiding the construction mechanism. These ancient builders were allowed to design the exteriors, and dress the outsides with their own styles of their messages of the dreams of God's greatness. People, showing unity. Allowing, communication, with Hieroglyph messages, around the world. Technology, that is still not understood, by some. We are still waiting to retrieve all the information so we can extract a deciphering method for the exterior design dictionary from Zifi Pinkiy.

As this technology is the exact same as what, we reference, as a Tesla coil today, but hidden inside, and made of pure 24 karat gold. These Giant golden coils have an advance internal wiring, with golden motherboards, that still to this day is not completely understood by all of mankind. As most of the future modern day construction was actually, stamped material, layer by layer, material by material, being printed, and cooled by high-tech material compounds streamlined by giant mega 6DRG printers.

These 6DRG printers will print, and make Israel's massive artistic buildings in three days or less again if needed. This giant building printer built the broken buildings in Israel, when they were destroyed in the past.

The Great Pyramid was so perfect, because a computer with a giant 6D material printer built the monuments, inch by inch, block by block, with selected hot molten material. As all the pyramids were printed moldings from a mega 3d advanced, printing computers. That is why modern, contemporary mankind cannot, duplicate the perfcotion of what a well programmed computer Zifi Crystal Skull can do.

As we confirmed, all the networking monuments have been pre-existing golden Tesla coils built internally. The internal guts are connected to the planets underground footings.

The planet connected as the (-Ground). All the internals of the monuments, had to be exactly the same interface network or the Motherboard planet project would not function, and cause chaotic electrical static charging disasters.

Placing the wrong data Zifi Crystal Skull on the wrong pillar co-ordinates, would render the network system non functional. The exterior static ionosphere would project random different illusionary facet energy static or what we call, normal, mother nature disasters.

This occurred if any of The Zifi Crystal Skulls were placed incorrectly. Each Zifi Crystal Skull would only function, at its designated, encrypted location. This balanced the planets gravitational field that is also invisible. Invisible waves, very powerful as, when lightning strikes.

If the wrong Zifi Crystal Skull was placed in the wrong pillar, there would be horrific weather crisis as tornadoes, whirlpools, quakes, and depression among-st humanity, from the wrong algorithm. Or weird, frequency code, microwaves, being discharged, would occur. It made good people do awful things. Some humans were affected by the invisible beams, and went killing or shooting innocent citizens. The humans in the way of the tiny beams, had dark matter blasted by a small invisible induction wave. All the affected humans would only remember that they blacked out. But the Devil made me do it. Were some of the criminals, excuses.

After many attempts, a certain anonymous Scientist finally, cracked the code on the location, and placement of the 12th Zifi Crystal Skull. Twelve dedicated remapped, nations derived from the discovery of the 12 Zifi Crystal Skulls home landmarks. The end result was the creation, and unity of (W.O.N.). World One Nation.

W.O.N., was finally diplomatically
contracted. As the instructions stated, with
peace on this planet, then other planets
will be awakened again, and only when all
the nations are at peace. Otherwise, the
message was that, the current man, will not
be allowed to the distant stars."

The Zifi Crystal Skulls begin to
again vibrate, and hum profusely as the 12th
skull is completely placed in its correct
pre-existing golden pillar triangular home.
The biggest 33rd Zifi Crystal Skull is deep
within the planets hidden tunnel to it's
internal hidden, crystal cores. Few
modifications would complete the final first
of many future calculations.

All the 33 Zifi Crystal Skulls
activate, and begin to illuminate different

colorful rays extensively. Each Skull,
starts vibrating, and hum different high
level frequencies, as all the completed
projects are at their final stages of
completion.

Each Zifi Crystal Skull, is in their
own assigned golden pillar. They are located
within their golden or crystal layer, and
start to emit their own sporadic laser
algorithm microwave outputs. This cuts the
air around them, perpetually with their own
coded frequencies. This effect makes a
soothing harmonious musical rhythm.

This effect begins to shake, and
vibrate magnetic speakers, and microphones
all around the world. All current
microphones contain little crystals within
the internal microphones to make voice

recognition possible. Cell phones are connected to the frequency. This is currently one of our possible present technological methods of recording to media devices. (Using Crystals.)

As the last Zifi Crystal Skull is in its final alignment, and placed on top of its golden pillar home, facing the correct direction to the North. More strange things begin to happen. Different tones begin to emerge, and vibrate pleasantness around the planet.

This controlled wave of a sensation causes a safe, united feeling around the world to all species. Certain birds, start singing a hypnotic tone. The Zifi Crystal Skulls make a strong sensation of peace among all habit-ants, and a warm feeling of comfort, and love, begins to harmonize, around the planet.

Surprisingly wolves begin to feed together with sheep, instead of attacking their prey, and Lions begin to eat flower, and hay like the ox.

The planet is now covered with an invisible, laser Hexagonal web networks, around the world. This humming sound makes a sensation for all humans to have a warm, and cool feeling of a pleasant child love within all beating hearts. Some Hexagonal webs, of illuminated laser lights, begin. All beams of laser lights connect the hexagon Zifi web from all The Zifi Crystal Skull locations.

This begins to make a visible shine of the hexagonal web network outside in the skies above. This effect is similar to a fabulous laser light show strategically connecting the world together. The Aurora Boreal is also, connects to the static field. The strategical center of the planet by the equator is where the blue 6th Zifi Crystal Skull is placed, and begins to shine a laser light in the night skies, of an image of the star of David on the ancient Hexagon Zifi network. Coincidentally, now, all humans, take a very deep, relaxing breath at the same time. The breath of life in the ionic field has a healthy, healing affect.

Then extraordinarily, a small sound of a heart beat commences in the air, and is heard by human brains. All heart beats of humans begin to pulse as one, and with the

special synchronized pumping expansion
rhythm.

A new cystic baby heart below the
Aorta rips in all human hearts, and then
immediately repairs, and creates a small
baby second heart in all human bodies. A new
loving healthy second heart emerges new
strength from our one heart. Giving
rejuvenating inspiring life to the extra
shocking rhythm of our new healthy hearts,
we now currently have. That was created from
the induction waves. All humans now have two
beating internal hearts.

This internal heart creates its own
defibrillator shocking good vibrations
around our inductions auras. Our blood, and
bones within the marrow, are boosted with

natural steroids, and elements that pleasure energetic life within us.

The sky where the center of David's star has an effect of a laser light emerging, and the essence of a 3D realistic beating human heart beats in the center of the image of the star of David. This heart, which is beating, is the health of the planet we live on, and is now being monitored by The Zifi Crystal Skulls controllers.

The planet is now brightly covered with the multi colored, illuminating hexagonal webs. This strategical hexagon web network laser light effect now covers the planet entirely, with a soothing brilliant hexagonal lighted web. Images of The Star of David, web begins to flicker different flashing beautiful lights all across the planet. The planet spins like a rotating hard drive. All life memories, capable too visually, see becomes a digital board.

This advance technology is now again awakened by humans, and now will be allowing many benefits of allowing an ancient Hexagon Zifi network to function. This connection will now, allow an ancient method of communications to the galaxies from the planet waves being created by the Zifi Hexagon-network.

This technology has been undisturbed for generations, and has many benefits as mind control of all different species. Humans can take total control, of the weather anywhere on the planet. Electrical human wormhole portals opening to be able to

travel around the universe on beams of
lightning bolts, created from the simple
atmospheric protons in the air. And many
more amazing effects that would unite, the
reconnecting, of mankind, with the galaxies
above.

Some archaeologists speculated from
scripture readings from the past, that this
amazing network gift would be achieved once
more, when a level of peace within
civilizations commences, and they all share
knowledge, not hiding anything from each
other. As the attempts to crack the code of
The Zifi Crystal Skulls, failed many times
over by many attempting humans. Outsiders
thought these men were crazy religious
freaks trying to crack a code that did not
exist.

The attempt of placing all the 33 Skulls in the correct golden pillar in order, and in their own designated Longitude, and Latitude location on the planet, while facing the correct direction on the planet in the exact spot, was the biggest code breaking ever known to mankind.

To this day, Scientist can, not figure out, and can only speculate, why all The Zifi Crystal Skull monuments were dismantled, and placed in 12 different regions. The Scientists messed up by not knowing the correct sequence time variables, and did not realize how important the order of placement would play a precise role in the hacking.

The Scientist, did not realize, at the time, that placing The Zifi Crystal

Skulls, in the wrong order, caused weather disruptions across the planet. After retrieving the data from the Pink Zifi Crystal Skull, less sequence attempts were tried, and less, disasters around the world occurred.

Finally, with the help from a guy, will just call The Ra., for now. Not even an elite team of Scientist realized how all The Zifi Crystal Skulls were placed in the wrong regions in their own designated pillars. The Scientist, and Archaeologist speculated, either the Crystal Skulls were distributed on an accident by other past species attempting to crack the code. Or, perhaps it was done, on purpose, to hide the powers, of The Zifi Crystal Skulls.

Most participants speculated
perhaps, to protect mankind, or a conspiracy
to just confuse humanity. Some speculated
that thieves that stole the parts, just
didn't know any better, and has changed
hands, numerous times, since on human knew
how to make it function. Most of the shells
were fake replicas, and did not contain the
mark of membrane, being genuine.

The thieves took special conducting
artifacts, not knowing what they were doing,
and making the planets secret puzzle more
confusing. As some of our special
Scientists were, taught by school of hard
knocks, and actually figured out the code
with third party outsiders.

Some Scientists have been supportive
to call the code cracker a hero. Some blogs

were bold enough to call him the Anti+Christ, a savior, and some even dared to call him the Devil in disguise. But, only time will tell, was said by some.

However, contrary to those statements, his information, and data, followed up with, when he was a child actually brought people together, to God, and showed how to crack a complicated code by other advance algorithm code methods, from historic calendars.

I know it sounds confusing, but as you are informed here, you will see what I see.

As the attempt to crack this code, and to create this amazing Zifi network with The Zifi Crystal Skulls, is not new, or the first attempt to try to make the system function. As when the Spanlizards invaded what is known as Mexico today. The invaders found the instructions on how to work The Zifi Crystal Skulls.

The instructions were projected from a red, and black Zifi Crystal Skull with horns on its head. But, BEWARE, not to say The Crystal Skulls, name out loud. The scripture retrieved, is what is now called the famous (Zifi Crystablo Diablocino Lucifer).

The original paper cloth scripture was burned, and never to be seen again. Until, we finally downloaded, the digital copy from Zifi Pinkiy. We know, now why the priests were scared of the images in the books they saw, as we now see them digitally, and we too would have destroyed them, if we were primitive people like the Spanlizards were, when they invaded parts of Califas, owned territories.

The images are actually scary.

As the placement code alignments, of The Zifi Crystal Skulls were attempted many times over with results of failure every time. It is finally a triumph for humanity to achieve all that is now achieved. As with unity, and trust in God, nothing is impossible for what humans can do as a whole.

The first attempt was a failure, as no one had the correct connections to do this type of configuration of the code without all the help of the United Planets of the Galaxies. They were also part of the enigma puzzle. There were many attempts by private sectors that found out about the technology, and of course these greedy humans, planed, and wanted to take over the world.

Eventually, the private sectors gave up as not all was revealed to them, making the Crystal Skull code, impossible to crack, and all deemed it a fluke myth. The truth would not be revealed, till the correct time was right, and would only be revealed, to good at peaceful heart. (According to legend).

As we now know why "Good at peaceful heart," is mentioned. The discovery of a tiny quad heart bubble is our second heart inside us, and is a good thing. As Zifi

Pinkiy, is now finally, putting out all that informative data. So, we felt the time has finally approached to reveal the secrets, and the time is today, right now at this hour.

We know the time is now since all the planets are aligning to reveal the hidden but visible secrets. If mankind was united, peaceful, and ready to believe, then we could accept the union, and phenomenal gifts of our unity.

The higher power would allow these amazing machines we discovered, to prevail in today's society. Mankind would know, and follow the safety rules of all the forgotten legends, and folk tales that were shared with ancient mankind. The unity of mankind was needed to complete the final connections of the puzzles. Many new attempts were given from donating groups, and eventually gave up for many generations from the greedy private sectors for the attempt of profit.

As always the private sectors finally gave up after many costly, failed attempts, and the private corrupted, sectors lost trillions of tax payers money to attempt to crack The Zifi Crystal Skull code. As all attempts to crack the code from the private sectors failed. With unknowingly coincidental Mother nature, disastrous accidents, would occur around the world, at the same time. With each failed attempt, more mother nature disasters, from the fluctuations.

Not one private sector even came close to making one of The Zifi Crystal

Skulls, hum a bit of a soothing vibrational sound, as when the real Bona Fide, good at peaceful heart code breakers cracked this code.

After many years of failed attempts, new teams of survivalist, were told of the secret possibilities that The Zifi Crystal Skulls could bring. The attempt, and search began, once more.

After several attempts of failure, by the chosen trusted public reality, televised show, of the Elite Scientific communities, felt frustration, and they almost, gave up. The volunteering Scientist on the broadcasted show, connected some of the puzzles by help of viewers, and by pure concentrated luck by some of the Scientists working for G.E.M..

Amazingly, and finally the code was
nearing to be unlocked, and the
preliminaries of the code were initially
cracked. The first correctly placed Zifi
Crystal Skull began to hum when it was near
the correct golden pillar. This was a large
break through, and now it was only a matter
of time, before the code would be cracked
completely. When some of the Zifi Crystal
Skulls were in place, humming, and lights
began enhancing the room.

The current G.E.M., Scientist, guest
speaker, begins, his speech by explaining
the live videos, and images of what is
happening around most humans on the planet
from the broad cast, satellite viewers.

A sleeping part of the brain awakens, and a laser viewer starts internally in the mist of our brains.

Images of our solar system begin to illuminate brightly above. Milky way clusters twinkle brightly, and so loudly with many colorful galaxies flashing rapidly beside us in a blink of an eye. We are now attached on the Galaxy Zifi network across the universe.

For a few seconds, so-called Hallucinations of ancient, but new to this generation, technology called V-images of Super Novas, and speeding stars above, and beside all of us, are screaming, with some relaxing full, 5 hertz, humming vibrations. The surrounding atmosphere is becoming, and feeling, as if we were scrolling our solar systems in a controlled method above our eye level view. The feeling of, cosmic AC1 rays of laser light beams, glowing & glittering, above the cool evening heavens, above us. In a refreshing format, that fills us up, with pure love.

As the current Executive Scientist from W.O.N., and G.E.M. continues:

" No Scientist ever tested the theory yet, but some speculated all young, and old human life had the same heart beat rhythms beating with the same rhythm of The Star of David that is illuminating brightly above near the equator. The few humans on heart monitoring machines. The statistic of this is correct, among those tested"

Suddenly a strong cool windy hypnotic breeze shake, and vibrate all the surrounding leaves in the trees, and bushes.

A low frequency, a robotic, vibrational sound, emerges in the air, from a new but ancient technology. That is called, the electronic Mother ship of Edem, and its Natural surroundings above, or (M.E.N.) for short.

The vibrational sound is so soothing, and is similar to water flowing in a perpetual river. The right ear, eight nervous system of the brain, gets a low tone frequency, and hears a vibrating sound, in the 5 Hz frequency level, emitting a sensation of nirvana to all species.

Special, energetic, sleeping endorphin fluid, is awakened in the brain, and splashes a refreshing fountain in all human brains, to a refreshing soothing feeling of comfort from the euphoric fountain of love, and life. Love, and new energized streams of life, now overflow, in all human brains.

Suddenly, there is a sonic boom, and the Zifi web wave frequency stops, and the frequency changes to a Moon 4 FM frequency.

Some human ears pop, opening blood vessels in many human ears, and brains. The sound effect, immediately kills, certain defective, attached tainted species.

A tiny voice begins to speak in all
breathing human ears, even the deaf with
ears can now hear.

"He who has ears let them listen,
and hear, our vibrating voice. Ladies, and
gentleman, we will shortly go live, with the
President of The World One Nations.

The President is now about to give
his emergency relief speech for the victims
families, which have encountered tragedy
with the ongoing horrific events from around
the world.

Thank you for joining us for our
first live event here at, Zifi Alpha Angel-
Ra Conference. Within the past few minutes,
we know, this has been a life changing
broadcast for some in our Galaxy Zifi

network. Your newly chosen President will now elaborate on this, phenomenons that are occurring around the world with many viewers that are contacting our emergency hot-lincs, with all similar or the same symptoms, and complaints.

The President will be explaining live after he joins us in a few seconds. Hopefully, all of you viewing, and listening to us, are well. We know all of this occurring may be a bit confusing, but bear with us, and we will explain.

We all here, at Grand Central are hoping all is well, and hope the induced are not one of the many individuals that rejected this broadcast, with a fatal, and erratic physical pop sound in the brain. Per say. I am told by my peers that many, viewers say that it has been very unpleasant for those that reported the incidents, before their deaths.

So we apologize to the masses for the temporary discomfort, and that ringing sound within your brain, or ears. The president will now begin."

The President now begins:

"Good morning all, the time is now 4:44 AM. Pacific standard time, and I thank all of you listening out there for choosing me as your world leader. As confusing as all these events have been, it may seem, and may start to sound bizarre, at it's highest. I will continue. Please, bear with me as I try to explain this newly discovered ancient phenomena. More then likely, you, and all

humans have or will be affected by the
procedure I am about to tell you, and I will
be upgrading your informational software a
bit, per say. I will be enhancing you with
these live updates, and tell you about this
top secret uncompleted phenomena we have
newly acquired, almost a century ago.

A scientific fact. All microphones
around the world have crystals internally.
Crystals are also, within the brain, and
tend to vibrate with tiny vibrational
frequencies, or dedicated algorithms.
Allowing, you the audience to see me, and
hear me speak. I thank, the planet viewers,
for helping us, crack an impossible code.
That would have never been able to have been
broken, without the help of the creative
young, and old. Giving us, those creative

opinions, which reshaped, how we cracked, this difficult Code.

Especially, thanking the wise older folks for assisting with the fantastic legends, passed on through generations, for this day to be remembered.

I am told that a 3-year-old with a 666-Terra hertz processor in her brain, assisted in the completion of these tasks, and still I am amazed that we as a planet now have unity, and can surely have no obstacles too small or big. As with this faith, and technology, we can now move mountains by our thoughts.''

The president clears his throat, and begins again:

" Myself, the President, and being a true Scientist by degree, and at heart, as well as a serious Chief in Commander, will now, progress, mankind, and inform any, and all of the top relevant secrets to update all the demanding public. I will begin by saying we have unfolded an ancient technology that we still are not sure who built it. Or we, are not aware of the true year or time it came from. Ever since we discovered these devices are the same, all over the world.

This ancient device, but newly discovered methods, on how to make some of the devices function, by our scientist is a phenomenon. Some data has recent revelations, known to mankind, that some secrets were discovered barely many decades ago.

Hitler, and Foreign terrorists, were some of our true awakenings. As Hitler held most of the blue prints that awakened the chase for this technology. This induction phenomenon has been running uncontrolled for centuries, and not monitored by any human, but just absorbing, and recording of man kinds emotions. We now, know that part of these phenomena are caused, from the wind blowing through the leaves of surrounding trees outside all environments, and certain alignments of masses. It creates a frequency, which weaves the ion fabric, and is what we are now in control of.

Hitler said, that he was the one who created the Skulls. Hitler stated, why he made the shape of The Crystal Skulls. Because they are just so cool, he stated. He could have put the computer in any box really, but these signified for mankind, and crystals are shiny. As you can see in the ancient crystals we were friends to children, and woman as we would be to any civilization that is going to comply with our civilization Classical Laws. The Software was uploaded into the diamonds, but the Crystal Skulls shape was created because they look so cool, and hold so much data. We knew he was not telling the truth.

We now know when the environmental ions are precisely aligned with hard masses around us, shape the outcome of numeric vibrations. Example. The floor, walls, phones, tables, a near moon, certain planets or any other material with, mass on certain frequencies, causes a ripple effect to conjure the phenomena in place.

I will explain how some of the
phenomenal work is created. There have been
experiments in the past, with electrical
currents passing through the sky, shocking,
and sparking humans. This phenomenon has
been occurring, since the beginning of time,
a push button ESP. The electrical currents
around us, are what gives positive powers to
some, but not all humans.

The energy is derived from the
clouds or heavens, sparking to the planet,
and then the human host. Exactly how a
synapse, in the human brain sparks
information. Mimicking, little lightning
bolts, on a micro level.

Some Scientists say helpful spirits
assisted to push mankind through decision

making, through a portal wormhole device.
Hence, the signs of the times are as simple
as, sound wave reactions similar to wind,
and sound effects that would be similar to
sounds around you, like a baby crying, dog
barking, someone laughing abruptly, a door,
closing, or as simple as a house with
cracking or settling noises. They're all
information precautions.

These natural, coinciding effects
induce mankind, never realizing the sleeping
brains within us. These phenomenons would
not be limited to electronic speakers that
have a magnetic base structure foundation.
The frame of the speaker system, and similar
coiled devices around the world would be
unknowingly induced by the effect.

The inductions, vibrating invisible wind frequency around us, would affect all internal coils in speakers around us vibrating a low buzzing frequency, and making the speaker cone bounce a bit. This effect would normally go, unnoticed to most human ears.

The low vibrations from the wormholes opening, a dedicated ion would normally be ignored, accepted, by dogs keen hearings. Humans that, could, hear the phenomena. They, could hear the vibrating signs around them, and be trancing into a zombie like zones. Posed with a mental blank face, and not even be aware of it.

I am sure it may have happened to you, when time sped up. And you wonder what happened? You feel either energized, or really tired, but with a huge loss of time, a day or so.

Most humans would hear the signs in the surroundings as an ear popping effect, sometimes bells, dogs barking, automobile horns or house settling popping noises, and other vibrating sounds at the right time of communication from our karma circle.

This static, noise or Holy Spirit would instantly warn us, of events in your surroundings, at all times, giving you signs, or danger warnings, of decision making for certain events. Some ancient scripture mentions that invisible ghosts or the Holy Spirit himself, is trying progress mankind. With warning signs, surrounding our environments.

This technology you see in front of your eyes, is similar to the outdated, but advance digital Glass wear. The glasses were exterior. As the Zifi technology your experiencing is borrowing storage, in brain cells. Causing, your many brain synapse receptors, to fire in harmony.

This would be the best way to describe the implemented sound signs, that this planets dimension, shares with us. These phenomena of signs, is happening around you right now as you are viewing, listening or reading the news e-card feed, miraculously in front of your eyes. The reality of the mystery vibrating signs, induce the mind. This in turn would cause the sound for a human ear to react, and vibrate our eardrums to a low pitch.

This human instinct we call, are
then translated, into sound effects, or
certain sensations, that would be similar,
to what animals, would naturally, recognize.
As the reaction of dogs barking when an
ambulance, fire truck, police or any
emergency siren, passing for a few seconds,
is a warning.

The emergency vehicles sirens, high
pitch sounds, traveling at high speeds to
emergency situations, is, always disturbing.
And heard from animals, keen hearings,
before a human does.

With these loud screeching sirens
bouncing air waves or electric horns that
are heard by dogs or other animals with keen
hearing is the similar effect in a way as

the wave of interception is transfused by
the elements of sound induction technology.

Humans, may have heard, this
amazing, 5 hertz tone from certain televised
channels in the past, that use exactly the
same frequency on some audio transfusing
commercials. This sound has the same effect
by vibrating human eardrums, obeying the
same laws of the infamous dark sided reality
of channeled television.

As you listen closely, the tone
around you is then suddenly, magnified to a
low sound that is miraculously an encoded
written code from an ancient language of
sound, like hieroglyphics, but in sound
technology wave format communicating
directly to the brain. This code is
encrypted, and invisible to the human eye,

but writes the human code to the brain, by
vibrating data to the ear drum, we call
sound.

But a different, realm, in the
manner, that it is transfused into the
understanding, that the brain only knows how
to decipher.

This is the same method a computer
programmer would write code for network
software. Not all human brains have the same
response, and will sometimes reject this
amazing human sound hieroglyphic code, that
is induced by this amazing code technology.
Some say it was written to kill demonetized
humans. But most humans are immune to the
sounds.

However, there are some heavy side effects to those that aren't affected by the sound. Unfortunately, some recorded side effects have been that certain ear drums get blasted from these tones. Causing, severe bleeding, to the ear drum. Flooding the membrane vessel channels with blood. Killing those individuals, with sensitive canals and, weak capillaries. Other reports have been of humans going deaf, tumors in the brain, and popped ear drums causing popped brain vessels, leading to possible death.

Great depression, and suicidal thoughts have also been recorded with some of these frequencies. The scary thing is that Mother nature, already reproduces these phenomenal distinctive buzzing sounds, before we even, tampered with the technology. At different, channels, of

uncontrolled frequency levels. Occurring,
naturally every day. If not controlled,
planets will have positive, and negative
side effects. Really depending where the
Milky way Galaxy is located in the universe,
exactly at that time. Similar, to the
physics, of the equator.

The buzzing sound is created
naturally in our current space, time, and
our location. Then gaps in trees, and low
pitch wind waves around us, working
together, in harmony, assist in the effect.
The one, static accords, that makes this
phenomena, possible. No one has ever put
these events together till all medical
clinics, and hospitals became a one
Government network called G.E.M. (Governing
Evolved Miracles).

This action by Scientist, and
Doctors were forced, and monitored to become
a one network entity, that progressed
medicine for human kind 100,000,000 fold.
This advance networking not only allowed
public access, but all world secret files
were made, and forced to be part of this
controlled network of G.E.M.. Human
existence depended on this for survival.

This great institute was created on
the count of survival from one huge plague
killing billions of people by the cosmos
above, and hybrid mosquitoes spreading, and
infecting mankind.

This mosquito that gives a
distinctive vibrational sound left mankind
no other choice but to unite or otherwise,
was the last straw for survival.

This poisoned hybrid mosquito was discovered to be created by cosmic intervention, from the location in the Universe our Galaxy spun, through.

The infections of this mosquito murdered possibly billions by killing humans indoors, and outdoors.

Humans thought the mosquitoes were the only thing killing humans, and thought to eliminate all mosquitoes to prevent mankind to perish. The real nature of the true disease that killed billions was yet to be discovered.

Leaders of the worlds worked hand on hand trying to discover why the human race was plagued so bad, and punished by God. At this point there were no secrets that didn't matter if there were no humans to keep secrets from.

Therefore, the Countries of the world splurged so much information to hopefully discover the cause of the plague.

This led to many secrets to be revealed, and caused some government officials to be killed by the public. Some of those corrupted government officials, Senators, National Security Advisers, committed suicide from the discovery of so much fraud from certain government branches.

There was still hope for human life with a mandated Open File Share program system in place by the governments that were

still alive in the new government branch of
G.E.M..

        This controlled progressions of
networking was the first peaceful break
through for humanity that would save many
human lives for the next future centuries.
Humans now know by 100% fact, that these
horrific events, also caused the extinction
of the dinosaurs, passing through this part
of the Universe, millions or maybe billions
of years ago.

        The newly mandated progressions
network, effect of G.E.M., immediately
discovered, and cured some cancers by the
public blogs working together, and notes
shared by the medical communities.

No one ever thought these great advances, and discoveries would be break troughs, from what we consider dead beat nobodies. Most discoveries were generated from 3rd world Country citizens, which we call nobodies. And from Countries we never bothered looking at, on a map.

Some of these advances were generated by, your normal analytical, teach yourself kind of human, that had little or no schooling. As those pupils, elders passing on the remedies of the past were awakened to share the knowledge. They were mostly taught by the school of hard knocks. Real life hands on training experiences came from the home schooled, that worked with diseased towns. The cure was simple, but not known to many. Until the network discovery added all the missing information, from a

man named, A.K.A.: RA. Written scriptures,
comprised by the missing frequency at hand,
allowed downloading, without pauses.

(The famous or some would say the
infamous Anti+Christ).

The first signs were as follow. The
answer of the cure was finally revealed. The
cure was simple. Do not be outside at
certain hours of the night. While this
Galaxy is in the Exacto, part of this
Universe. The alignments of our solar system
would pass high levels of harmful, and
undetectable by most equipment, large
radiation fields to bounce off aligned
planets on certain calendar days of the
certain years. Repetitive, clockwise
rotation.

Thus, making it impossible to be immune as the radiation would melt capillary receptors, immediately, to certain humans, dismissing the radiation, into the blood, of the infected. Therefore, killing them quickly. Or worse, suffering, a slow death, on a future day. Low energy outcomes. Depending the radiation flares, the infected got exposed to.

This in turn, also created, and affected the newly hybrid mosquito, allowing indoor, sheltered deaths as well. This in turn has confused mankind where the disease came from. When it was actually coming, from cosmic rays, from the galaxies, far away.

The Bible, coincidentally had a similar story, with Angels of death, wiping out evil branches of mankind. The story says, that a few Angels were going to allow death to people who were outside on certain hours of certain calendar days of the year, when God got tired of the sinners repetitiveness. Some Mayan Hieroglyphs called it the day of the dead, and was misunderstood.

The Mayan ancient calendar, as well as the informed ancient calendars, has, the same warnings. These were warnings to mankind of what century, and certain years to be concerned with. Spelling out certain decades, of time, when the celestial, radiation radiated. Only when our Galaxy would be aligned, or near a Galaxy in the far reaches of the Universe, called, Tic Toc. There living beings meditate an induction affirmation, to trance the near by humans wired body, negative waves.

As the instructions of the ritual to
be safe was indicated by the good book, or
as ancient calendars, also advised, and
predicted of the warnings.

Instructions would be, for the
followers of God, and they would sprinkle,
certain animal blood, to inform, the flying
Angels, not to enter their dwellings, with
the curse. The testimonies, show the Angels
agreed to not enter the followers dwellings.
And, this allowed death to others, but not
in the dwellings of the followers.

As strange as a story from the Bible
goes, sprinkling certain, animal blood was a
true deterrent to mask the radiation or

divert, the mosquitoes, as a cellular
filter.

Finally, the discovery of radiation,
that only occurred on certain nights was
revealed. Many billions of unfortunate
deaths had already occurred.

The blood of certain animals
sprinkled in areas or covered by the blood
from certain animals would deter the
radiation levels.

It also, affected, mosquitoes, and
were deterred completely from being in the
area from certain types of blood being
sprinkled around the dwellings.

However, if people were under any
shelter, while the cosmic radiation rays

were emitted to the planet, the individuals would not be in harms way, while under the shelters protection. As the structure saved the occupants from the exposure, but not the mosquitoes, bite.

What made it more confusing was that some humans would take weeks or months, before they collapsed, and died. Making the cause of death diagnoses, as a heart attack, or inconclusive.

As some humans would die on the spot making the cure, more of a challenge. As oddly as it sounded, these were true coincidences. As the translations of the Bible were written histories, of future, and past events. We still hear from the medical community, and we wonder, were these people chosen to be allowed to die intentionally.

Since, it was written with warnings from the past, and may have been fate, from the scriptures.

Since it has now happened, it is mankind's fate to die, and succeed, and then to unite the rest of the world, or perish to be extinct as the dinosaurs were once taken.

Most of these theories, and discoveries were from an inventor by the name of Ra., who studied cultures, and detail integrated system levels of telepathic, and astrology characters. Of course no one listened to him as he was preaching before the billions of deaths, and at the time he sounded crazy. He claimed this radiation field effect would surely, infect most of the planets, and only few were safe. However, when the planet rotated,

and was facing the other side of the
radiation field, the world would be in
jeopardy once again. Infecting more exposed
humans.

The Ancient, followers of God, knew
when humans would not be allowed out of
their residence, with this new discovery,
and Bible history.

20% of the best medical
professionals also, came through, with other
break through discoveries, and cures for
humanity, with the new implemented medical
network system, of G.E.M..

These new developments turned, and
changed the world of plagues that would be
killing human lives for centuries if not

implemented by a one government nation of
G.E.M..

On the plus side of these phenomena
of sound technology, there were also,
positive effects of this amazing sound that
was labeled as, the T buzzing sound. The
sound, that greatly differed on different
humans, for the good.

This amazing effect could also bring
euphoria to those that are fortunate enough
to be able to tune into the correct
frequency levels or direct algorithm
implosion. Some humans have said this very
similar discovery of the euphoric buzzing
sound would have been imagined to always be
playing in the Garden of Edem. This delight,
and curse of this technology are similar to
having a switch turning on, and off. The

switch is tuned to a euphoric soothing
vibrating, rush in the Basal Ganglia of the
brain.

In turn, turning the switch
frequency off, and tuned into a higher
channel frequency would give the chaotic
vibration of thoughts that put you into the
garden of evil. These on, and off membrane
switches were mandated to be controlled from
one, and only one discrete big chief in
command of the T networking system from
G.E.M..

To bad for our greatest grand
parents that got us shunned from the Garden
of Edem, and has made us limited to the
euphoric harmony from the Garden of Edems
beauty. Still uncertain for some, but
permanently discharged from entering the

gates, and doorways to eternal euphoria for others.

We all know why the Great boss above got angry at our Greatest Grandparents, and made humans lose the chance to be in Heaven with him, until the day of judgment day 89.

Jesus was a relative. The fabric of life continues.

Some Translations, & parables from the good book:

The Bible.

THE SPIRIT OF THE HOLY ONE TESTIFIES

WITH OUR ELECTRICAL, MAGICAL THING WE CALL,

A SOUL, A SPARK WITHIN. THAT WE ARE THE
ANGELIC LIGHTED, SPIRIT CHILDREN OF OUR
GLORIOUS AWESOME, RIGHTEOUS LEADER WE CALL
GOD... O.M.G., SOME DENY IT, BUT KNOW IT,
TO LATE. Lighted induction.

                                   Similar to
Romans 8:16.

        We are the true children of God's
seeds, as the gift from God blesses the
breath of life, that, we, all are connected
to. The infrastructure of the Zifi network
connection we are on.

        This new discovered technology
changed the world of Scientist views, that
led all Scientists to believe in God. God is
the one that permanently allowed the off

switch for humanity, and the euphoria by creating a chemical compound that was embedded into the forbidden fruit of knowledge.

Like a cancer or virus that merged to your binary DNA. God made rules, warned, and told our beyond Great, Grandparents not to eat this fruit, and God allowed Adam, and Eve to indulge in life, and eat anything, and everything. But, were forbidden to consume the one embedded, and cursed Fruit of Knowledge, that contained transparent Dark Matter. It is like a parasite. The chemical reactions are emitted in the air, and bam, you are hypnotized.

This introduced human kind into a chemical that was permanently woven directly to our DNA's, muscular hearts, and mended

into every generation from the weaving
bloodline of humanity.

Hence, our DNA. has the fruit of
knowledge compound embedded to our DNA,
permanently from the day our Greatest
Grandma & Greatest Grandpa, ate the
forbidden Fruit of Knowledge.

This curse came from the tempting,
juicy, forbidden fruit of knowledge. That
was a lie from a dark sided snake. The juice
from the fruit has adhered tightly to our
base foundation, and has blended a
compounded effect in our DNA.

This transducer chemical compound
that entered into our DNA made the blind
Adam, and Eve see, and wake up to their

odors, and nakedness, and all, the promised curses that followed.

Give me a moment so you will understand as I do. Let's just say that half of the humans, came from an evolving specie, of a form of a monkey and/or lizard. As certain past scholars have portrayed as it to be. Evolution.

So there are about half of humans or less that came from an, evolving, learning lizard or monkey that has been evolving, and enriching their own lives, from the inception of the planet. No morals. Like mosquitoes do.

The other half of humanity, as scholars have recorded this history to be true, as there are higher powers, and one

leader for the higher powers to continue the
future. What if, not aliens, but a supreme
sovereign leader, the big real king of
little kings, the one that is called, A
Savior. Taking care of humanity, with a
genuine plan, which works.

When God made the Universe,
evolution took place as humans have evolved
for centuries. The only difference, God did
make the pure creature of Adam, and Eve, and
allowed, their siblings to occupy the
planet. As subordinate, theories of evolving
monkeys, and lizard people are on the
planet, and have also, evolved. Making the
slow evolution of life from the copied woven
5D prints, into the fabric of Adam, and Eve.

This hypothesis, was challenged, and
the records of these breeds were completed,

and now we know, they are among us all. The evolution continued, and the breeds have been mixing, as they are now. Evolving, into our leaders plans, as written. Without God, man will not have absolute morals.

Not all testimony scrolls were found, till the first Zifi Crystal Skull guided us to their locations. The scrolls even warned us to never leave our guards down from the Devil. The Devil has, and is trying to take over the planets, forever. As the Devil, currently has, the lease consents, on this planet.

Or until the Devils next meeting with God. And he has a no rule policy for human life. So the Devil avoids this meeting, until he has enough souls to attack, and try to take over God's realms.

As the Devil sees, humans as mere tools, for the future fight with God. The Devil will tempt you many times, and will never stop, attempting to. Until you become his soldier tool, for this life. And his soul tools for, the next life to fight against God.

We are, thankful to God that he still waits patiently for our cooperation. Mankind scientifically knowing now, that we are born cursed in a way. With human beings, still being structured, to a natural infant mind stage. As sad as it may sound, it is the truth.

Mankind will never be able to get to that natural frequency of The Garden of Edem again without the aide of advance technology. Human lives, demand for something so powerful, that will hopefully,

and permanently shake that diseased chemical
compound off our DNA

Allowing us to walk into a great
vibrational frequency that will give us that
natural blinding, of a theta brain wave
effect while awake permanently.

Unfortunately, this effect for
humans has always been impossible to never
be able to get to that true ultimate
functional euphoric brain wave state again
while we are awake.

UNTIL NOW! Today's date, this very
hour."

Chingar Federickostuven, mentioned,
to the scientific community, who attended

the concerning Quantum Physics seminar, in the past. History showed from Zifi Pinkiy.

Years later, to a dedicated group of Scientist, were allowed to meet, on Cholola Mountain. Chingar quoted, and said something in regards to the spirit realms.

"Humans, with a human membrane, who becomes induced, and involved in sci-fi or real science of facts, that are substantiated with hard facts that prove methods. Becomes convinced, that there is, a greater frequency of an energy spirit, a ghost. Entwining a soul, in the policy of the parallel worlds. We know, that an invisible being, a ghost, that will be vastly knowledgeable of right, and wrong or superior to that of any creature. God. The transparent connections that makes the

inevitable occur. Intertwined, with a Godly
force, that makes dedication to the
invisible thought of natural, and paranormal
miracles or phenomena. A subconscious
awakening, of light and sound. Answering the
conscious minds requests. Miraculously."

The president drinks, some water.
Clears his throat, then begins again.

"Since 1923 Scientist discovered
that the planets axis can be controlled by
underground controls within the core of the
planet. These, secrets have been patented
with confidentiality trade secrets, and have
never been disclosed to any human. Except
the Scientist, that were working on it in
1943, and my team.

Called;

(Zifi Crystal Skull, download, project).

This opened up this newly found discovery, and apparently is more ancient then most have ever dreamed possible. Still to this date, no Scientist has been able to place the true age of this technology. I will continue, and explain, since our new world, now, has no secrets.

Part of the technology is using series of turbulence disruption crystal resisters. They were used in ancient civilizations, before, with strategically placed golden Tesla coiled structures. The pyramids on the planet or other hidden structures with these golden coils, were made specifically for this connection around the world to be connected together, and closing the static loop.

The Scientists working on this project have, been able to modify the planets motion, and movement for years now. And have perfected the air flow through channeling in certain clouds in the atmospheric air above us.

We control the weather by using certain lighted beams, with electrified gem stones that are used to bounce brilliant lights into the sky. As advanced as we have been able to achieve this great power, is still so amazing that we have even been able to control the planets weather better then imagined. This technology has been controlled to have the effect of creating dark gray clouds to channel rain in one very small area.

As small as a centimeter if decided to be deployed by the user. This precise technology used by these Scientist could fill your cup full of water to the rim with rain water, and then stop with a click of a button, and not spilling any drops out of your glass.

We got so good that this process could be done while your holding the glass cup out of your moving vehicles window, while your driving at 100 M.P.H.. But, we are still infants compared to what can be done with the final alignments of the galaxies, and The Crystal Skull puzzles, we have pieced together. We as a United Nation

of the Planet will discover the
undiscovered, great benefits together.

This jump advancement of what these
advancing Scientist have created from Mother
Natures Elements wasn't really theirs. But,
just copied by intellects of history, that
awakened this sleeping technology. They were
able to use lasers, and different brilliant
colored illuminating crystal gems to
illuminate the night sky, or to cause
violent tornadoes, hurricanes, from 1 mile
to 1,500 mph winds, from special diamond cut
lighted crystal gems. We dared not to pass
those miles per hour as it would cause to
much damage. We fear it could go much faster
then 1,500 M.P.H..

The Scientists were ordered to stop the experiment with wind motion since it was destroying paths, and deemed very dangerous.

We could knock down any missiles like a fly if ever deployed to our nation with this technology. And then send their own missals back with tornadoes.

The mixture of crystal gem colors can create a frequency to generate a soft but steady breezes, through trees, and shrubs. Creating a bounce of natural, and equalized frequencies to pass through the air. Pinkiy tells us we could deploy water as small as a needle in size or as big as Africa in size, if desired. With the correct software added to potentiating low, level voltage outputs, together with certain Zifi Crystal Skulls.

This effect would make electronics, and surrounding speakers in households to emit an inducing sound, that made a circular sound perimeter around you.

These phenomena can be identified similar to a dedicated wireless fax transmitting to a certain phone number any where in the world. This in turn would also have pros, and cons, by being able to send, to certain individuals around the world a buzzing, 5 hertz mega watt frequency, to the right frontal lobe hemisphere of the brain.

A buzzing sound. As similar to a dedicated I.P. address or a cell phone number to each type of individuals with a device. But directly to the brain. Also, similar to the phone you own, or the latest in Zifi Bio wear Tech Gear. Having the cell chip directly in your hand, or the evolving SKAT integrated units. This new technology will allow making calls with your thoughts.

The powers would be able to transduce a transmission of a hypnotic pain or an indescribable relaxation at the same time with controlled frequency, of a DNA. You could also, say that this method, this new technology, would work as similar to a WiFi cloud, a hot spot if you may, a tethering effect, a Light flash data wave, or a cloud floating in the air above, and any Internet network you are familiar with.

You would be able to hear the noise around you in the clouded background as the sound vibrates a faint water sound dripping into a pond or knives cutting your eardrums, depending the signal broad-casted. This causes an invisible current of gaseous rippling wet waves to bounce in the cloud you are in, and appear into every breath we inhale.

The sound is so abstracting that you can move the code around you, and feel the Terror around you in the air if the switch was turned on, to a different transducer, disturbing frequency channel. As thoughts become words, and their frequencies, can cut like a double sided sword.

These amazing vibrational words can be like a double edged sword twisting ions, like never before. From the figure 8 shape vibrations.

We have deemed this technology to be still too powerful for mankind if used incorrectly. We now know that the Devils could use it to open a portal to their dimensions, and then to this world bringing the demons to the sister planets or galaxies near by. We deemed this technology to be kept secret, and be dismantled, since it could be used as an evil weapon if used incorrectly for evil.

We speculate, and have recorded transmissions that the Devil's were successful enough to open a gateway in 1922, somewhere in the 1950's, 1971, and a transmission was recorded on You-tube in 2012. We have confirmation of a channel frequency, transmission to one of our devices years after the 1st broadcast, and

we were ordered to keep this information, a
top secret.

We have reason to believe, some
alien beings were possibly, transported
trough, and are living in existence among
us. We speculate they are probably building
their legion, since the 1922 transmission.
According to statistics, and interviewed
witnesses. A small gateway black hole
radiated in Mexico skies. An abnormal
sighting, but we now understand the
phenomena. We do not know if they were
friends or foes that got in.

Instead the limited partial devices
were dismantled in the 1900's. Supposedly
the system, the 3 Zifi Crystal Skulls, we
had at the time, and all the golden
artifacts were dismantled, and distributed

to a hidden secure location, underground, so
no human, or demon could ever use it.

As time passed there were mysterious
natural deaths to most men in the
organization, and in time this technology
had become forgotten.

The end of the world, and the
sharing of this technology of Open File
Share program allowed us to retrieve the
forgotten system, and attempt to master the
control panels. Some Scientist after
significant studies have concluded there are
still disturbing developments of all the
discoveries that have been unfolding. They
said they probably need two lifetimes till
all the discoveries will be understood by
humans.

Also, with our new found administration of G.E.M., some directors, and scientist have suggested that the air you breath is also, a written code of oxygen nano particles that is embedded with codes in the air for life. The breath of life. You need to have the breath of life to give the breath of life. The connections, to all humans have been what some Scientist label the air code as oxygen.

This ionic code connection is what connects everyone to one big networked cloud through the air around us all.

Scientist theories, that this connection is how we are all wired together with software that is written with ionic nanobot technology. From what they call the Flower of Life software or similar to a predecessor computer network with wireless technology. This connection we share is a common huge network that is controlled by the higher power or Scientific creator that is all around, and within us. Oxygen.

We are like peripheral devices that run on one connected channel that was strategically placed, and programmed on purpose, to do that of what we do, and are doing now. The plan he has for us.

Miraculous our creator has set us to run our brains with integrated wiring that upload, and download to the big server above us, as we blink awake or in our sleep. Upload, download, as you are blinking. Signals of what we are doing at this second are uploading, and downloading like a wireless device, by every vibrating blink of our eyes.

This method that all humans are connected to a God device, would make, Scientists frown, not believing. Some of those scientists were hoping to see a different light but as more advancements occur every day we now know there is a biological server per say all around us watching, and allowing us, life till the time line is changed by hidden sins, that the big man above, at all times can see, us. You better not pout, I am telling you why. You know the rest. Humans are proof of this. By the codes that we inhale, and exhale while uploading, and downloading, data, and these occurrences are every second.

We are all bonded together by the code, and we provide all this information, on a dedicated big cloud server above a wireless coded breath of life. This invisible surrounding of thoughts we emit into the air around you, is also, considered a circle within our auras if you may. And all binary celestial conscious existence is the same connection that all humans have in common. Of course only the humans, that are alive, and sharing the networks breath of life connection. Without air, you are severed, to the connection. No wireless ionic connection, means death. Unplugged.

One other startling, and disturbing discovery is that we would not of ever shared with humanity this secret, but G.E.M. manifesting the truth to the people. Will do so.

The secret is very scary in a way for privacy or evil sinners as this device we eventually found, is able to see throughout the hosts eyes of every human, regardless where there at.

Even deep underground, underwater or in space. We still have not found the portal to see through God's or the Devil's eyes.

The monitoring server is able to see through all our eyes, and be attached wireless, and circuited with the invisible electric current meters from our own pre-programmed eyes, and brain coils. Scientists have records, and opinions of this connection that has been verified by many hours of monitoring since the 90's.

These rumors, have been proved, and is scientifically has been proved, that it exists. This being a true fact, as you are uploading all your thoughts of information by waves of induction. It does make sense we all share, this connection, and are all united, UN-doubtfully, but out of our conscious reach.

Unfortunately the hybrid demons that are left on this planet weave into some of humans anger, and log into the human host, and cause mischievous malice. We still have yet to discover more treasures, that God has put into this miraculous device. We also, call this device, (The God Flower Cell of Life).

The God Flower Cell of Life, is as a wireless, microorganism connector. A queen bee, a virus, for the brain to implement their own thoughts. And controlling thoughts for the host, by using the followers different Hz frequency DNA code. Similar to remote control on a computer. Thus, the higher power controls all in harmony if he wishes. Knowing we are controlled by the human connection. We all have the breath of ionic life that proves we have one destined higher evolution of power.

Air, and ions, being the conductor that connects all life together sharing ions in a molecular structure breakdown we call oxygen. Hypothetically, the scientific community has agreed the one in charge of our wireless signal transmitted by air, conductors, and telepathically have similar bonded connections.

This concluded enough facts that there are a higher power that gave us limited knowledge, since our bodies are too fragile for the power that is slowly emerging on our tested volunteers.

All subjects are now, tranced super humans, from the rhythms provided by The Crystal Skulls music selection that we downloaded. These subjects are an elite group if you may, that have, attempted to be, and are experimenting with the development of the device of The God Flower Cells of Life, programming. The Scientific community has concluded with this new technology provided to the scientific community, and has concluded all their facts.

With these devices, Scientists could even be able to channel in on any left human eyeball, and see what the human host is seeing. This has proved to the lucky scientists that guessed what this technology could do but, on a greater level. We were able to tune in, and see what human beings were doing through the hosts eyes as a shared monitor screen, if you may. That is why you see history leaders or historians normally are covering one eye.

This in fact has proved, there are capable benefit methods for us to use this technology in good, and bad ways, and has proved that there is a higher power, actually monitoring, and recording our lives.

We got so advanced that, not only were they capable of seeing, through your eyes with the God Flower Cell of Life. But, while connected to one of The Crystal Skull network, we would be able to use a digital phone, like devices anywhere in the world, and still see you. The chosen Scientists were watching through your eyes for days, from their programmed cell phone devices.

Talk about how everyone thought it was their phones that were tapped, but their brains, and eyes were actually the way we saw humans in action. Some scientific viewers had side effects, and thought they were you, the actual host. Since the Scientists saw, everything, you saw through your eyes. Live TV viewing. Amazing.

Seeing your nose, and arms in front, and hands like it was their eyes. If you do not believe it, I will Have Adam another top Scientist, explain.

As ironic as it is, our expert Scientist in this field is also, named Adam. He will now explain. Thank you for listening or absorbing the waves we have induced by the Zifi Crystal Skull Network, and The God Flower Cell, induction transmissions."

Adam begins to cough, clears his throat, and picks up his cup of water, and starts to drink a cup of water with a thirst that was still not quenched after 2 cups.

Adam now says:

"If we were to drain a human of all their liquids, we would see a crystal form of powder. Yes crystal, like salt particles. Memory is a very small crystal liquid element in our brains that stores data images of your life, like silicon on micro-chips. That is why crystals, rocks, silicone, wood, and everything that has mass, can, and will get vibrations, that record in their own unique way. Some elements are easier to extract, the stored information. Some other elements, as U.S.B. sticks, crystal antennas, liquid, or anything that can shine a lighted surface, can record differently.

Imagine what the higher power one sees, through your eyes? What a show that would be. The fact there is the one higher power that knows all, and sees all, is what

we now believe from this technology, and
conclude there is a one creator, we call,
and praise, known as God.

Thank you God.

We were created as a plan, that is
why you are here reading this, and being
informed of the new technology break
through, from your reception code in the
brain. As were connected, and know that we
are being watched.

Forget all privacy regulations that
the Devil's lawyers made you believe. As we
were naked when we were born, and our
crystalline brains, have been recording
since first conception. All the tiny like
crystals inside your body have been
recording, and the vision images can now be

extracted from the brain with this device.
Synapse fire a spark of light with every
thought. Images on a lightning bolt inside
your brains core.

Yes, a spark of light, so small that
only the power of the flesh God gave us to
endure. Packed up with bright data, etching,
and storing into the data cells in the body.
If a human loses, a body part, certain parts
of the crystalline cell memories are lost.
The human will never be aware of the memory
loss, since they will not remember or miss
those memories of the past.

Important data is stored in the
middle of the brain, exclusively, and reruns
of garbage data, goes deep in the bone
marrow. The crystalline memory cells, are
smaller than nanobot technology, and are

hard to miss unless you have or know the Map of Memory Streamline. The feet marrow gets the most data junk. While behind the eyes, has system life support data. The autonomous memory brain cells, provides life support breathing.

The report came from mostly atheist scientists that are ashamed, and most of them fell down starting to cry profusely, screaming why they did the things they did in the past. As I was embarrassed to ask as I still know I have been a good person to humanity to all my brothers, and sisters."

Adam takes a deep breath drinks more water, and continues.

"I will read the report from the ex-
atheist, Scientist conducting the
experiments, that are as follows.

My name is Darwin Curiel, and we
have concluded, from all Scientific
communities a report. And have diligently
concluded, that the proof of human life, has
been created with endings of a higher power
that obviously exists, and keeps most of
life's chaos in order. The discovery of
this advanced IG-viewer, was actually found,
in Mexico's biggest pyramid hidden under a
giant mountain, that has opened the eyes of
the Scientific community.

Hence, knowing this new data, and
having the means on channeling into every
uncooperative human vision, through their

own eyeballs on this planet, is terrorizing, and amazing.

Even situated from the other side of the world has made us wonder when, and if we are going to be lucky enough to meet our creator at least once again. More then likely we have had contact with him many times, and us being so, naive never knew that he has contacted us through mediums or his breath of life.

As we hope our loving father slightly kisses us once more, and forgives our stupidity, and iniquities.

We hope that the great one gives us at least a light of inspiring touches, of his genuine love. As some of us that our lucky enough to inhale, and exhale, are lucky enough to feel the love that he brings to those who he has forgave, and those that beg for forgiveness, and are blessed with his touch of joy. Without God, as our higher power, morals, respect, and righteousness of good over evil will never exist.

This in turn would produce pure evil chaos for those that do not believe. As some of us in the Scientific communities, and atheists, did till we looked through the eyes of 10,000 humans. Even catching high ranking officials being criminals whenever their reflection in a mirror was around. Being able to see whose eyes we looked through, or finding them through building addresses as they viewed the streets they were on.

Knowing where the host lived, and
watching many disgusting things, and habits
of humanity. All these events were recorded
on MyeyeItube, as part of the G.E.M.
agreement.

We advise to adults, what you are
about to view would incarcerate, and bust
senators, presidents, teachers, fireman,
police, Judges, or even plain John ,and Mary
Doe. We watched people getting murdered,
and many good hearted individuals with the
pure breath of life, that God righteously
gave to them. Seeing through the eyes of
little babies as soon as they connect to the
breath of what we call the Breath of Life
Connection.

Some stories, of historical life,
have assumed a life of doing evil, and good

has been meaningless to their minds. The
evil human retarded demons have done as
their fancy strikes them as they take human
souls captive, and are somehow, manifested
by different demons.

Doing evil to others, and not caring
of punishment from laws. As the current
punishments are light, and unfulfilled to
their souls. As the evil retarded ones or
what we now know have been labeled as weak
minded demons on our filing system. As the
(retarded ones), or classified as (The
Y=O..O's, Y=O..O's.). Y=O..O's, for short.
The demons assume that they are to smart for
societies, organized crime preventions, of
manufactured mandated laws.

The laws were created to protect the
majorities safety. The violators do harm,

and cause years of agony to unfortunate, unforgiving souls. God uses the demon humans as examples. And puts them on the news so human eyes may see the chaos if humans don't change. One day God will not, turn his cheek any more, and remember he will remove your name from his book of life, and his list, without abidance.

Unfortunately, for all we do not know, if you may have already been removed from the book he made to allow access to the other real gateway to Eden. God will procure his covenant, promises of good, and bad. Historical documents from historically written covenants, that have shown this is a fact.

Thank you so much for allowing me to speak the report to you, as we know, we are all connected to the big server above, and are like wireless phones, connecting to the server. I now welcome, and we now, bring back your current leader, the President of The United Planets. Thank you again"

The President clears his throat, drinks, some water, and begins speaking.

" In the past this technology has been unstable, and is uncontrollable at times, since we are still learning how to use it. The peripheral devices still overheats on

us. And we knowing, we do not have the right to peer into human eyes. Probably, limits us to making it work all the time. The few weeks of the eyeball viewing we

saw through the eyes of random humans was inspiring. This has allowed us to see

events that were live, and happening in
today's lives.

In conclusion, and unfortunately our
accidental discovery of this artifact, and
how we channeled into the bridged software,
with the super computer. When we connected
with the super computer, it malfunctioned,
and blew up as a few previous times before.

This occurred, while trying to
replicate a machine that could televise a
broadcast to billions. Unfortunately, there
is a metal in there, that is a golden
tablet, with material not known to man, on
this planet. As we have called it the
Supreme Man Metal, (S.M.M.).

Normally, Since we can not copy the
metal here on this planet, makes it

impossible to completely replicate these machines ourselves. Pinkiy does not always give the data in order.

Rumor has it that not all the technology was lost in the fire in the 20's as history showed us that a man named Tesla stumbled on these secrets from a pyramid cave he would explore in his home country, when he was a young lad.

Tesla never told anyone about what he saw in those caves, but got a mindful of images that changed the face of this planet forever. When Scientists were taking the machine apart to replicate the technology, the machine had a self destruct button of some sort, and infused itself causing an explosion, and destroying all files that were lost, and either stolen by top agents

during the fires, and explosions in the
20's. This is a futuristic devise that is
here in our present time, and we really do
not know what year we are in anymore, as
this technology is so advance.

We will never know who were the host
that created these super computers that we
were replicating, and working on in the
past. Hence, we now know that we are not by
chance, or by evolution, but created for a
higher purpose by a higher power that is
still far from most humans grasps. We will
try with great effort to recreate what was
lost.

Therefore, we now believe, and know
there is a God. Thank you God for allowing
us to follow you, and by you touching our
souls, and awaking a glimpse of what you

see. Please forgive us for all our sins,
since humanity has done uncountable sins.
Thank you.

Silence occurs for 3 seconds.

Then all of a sudden a wave length
interrupts the frequency, and you hear Rock,
and Roll music with a beat of Hip Hop, and
steel metal beats in the induction waves.
The beat starts.

Yo ooo, yo oooou, yo o o o o, yoo o
yo o yo yo yo o o oooo, yo o yo o yo o o o,
yo o yo o yo o o o o.   Yo ooo, yo oooou, yo
o o o o, yo o o yo yo yo o o oooo, yo o yo o
yo o o o, yo o yo o yo o o o o.   Yo ooo, yo
oooou, yo o o o o, yoo o yo o yo yo yo o o
oooo, yo o yo o yo o o o, yo o yo o yo o o o
o. Yo ooo, yo oooou, yo o o o o, yo o o yo

yo yo o o oooo, yo o yo o yo o o o, yo o yo o yo o o o o. Hrrrreerer, herererreeerer.

Then a loud team of soldier demons break in to the Presidential Control room. The numbers are great, and easily annihilate all the security in the building. As they arrive through worm holes through the Zifi networks UN-programmed firewall. The Captain enters the control room, and kills the Presidential leader, and all his body guards. The demons, with their leader, Demon-Ice Eyes, takes over the control device.

You now hear the leader by the name of Demon-Ice Eyes, and begins to say on the induction air waves.

"This is only a dream on cloud 3, there is no God, and especially there is, no Devil. Except Devil drinks, 3 times the caffeine, and caffeine is good for you, it gives you energy, it does not kill you.

Awaken, and obey the viewing or television broadcasts. Buy Devil monster drinks. Know, you immoral atheists, that your leader, is Satan, forever. And obey your current future leader."

The backup, Un-tranced, Marines, and Air force elites, immediately realize the President is dead, and see what is happening from their video feed from the control room, and are already dispatched to the Capital of the world. A 711-sky jet saucer arrives while Demon-Ice Eyes is still talking, and the jets drop particle laser frequency

missiles, and blow up the Capital with all
the demon portal holes still open.

The marines had to sacrifice most of
the parts of the control device room, before
the mutants entered the planet with a
militia of mutants. The device is lost once
more, and the signal is lost all over the
world. The hexagonal web is now diminished,
as a loud humming sound vibrates across the
world.

All of a sudden, in movie theaters,
and certain churches that had gold plating
inside, their buildings all around the
world, begin to vibrate chaotically. The
vibrations went all the way to golden
bedroom walls, and vibrated what felt, like
non stopping force. But the floors do not

move. Miraculously, everything is still in
tact.

Then a last vocal signal is induced
by the air frequency, and an Angelic vocal
spirit sound vibrates passages from within
the walls all around the world, vibrating a
tranquil smooth humming sound with a voice
that cuts all air wave molecules, and begin
to vibrate a powerful (hummmmm), sound, and
the following words are vibrated.

THE SPIRIT OF THE HOLY
ONE TESTIFIES WITH OUR ELECTRICAL, MAGICAL
THING WE CALL, A SOUL, A SPARK WITHIN. THAT
WE ARE THE ANGELIC LIGHTED, SPIRIT CHILDREN
OF OUR GLORIOUS AWESOME, RIGHTEOUS LEADER WE
CALL GOD... O.M.G., SOME DENY IT, BUT KNOW
IT, TO LATE.

Similar to
Romans 8:16. The vibration stops, and all
species way of previous, lives behaviors
return to their normal, circle of life.

Any human that is logical in
science, and knows Quantum Physics, has an
opinion of the spirit worlds. Anyone, a
human, who becomes seriously involved in the
accomplishments of logistics, or facts, that
are documented, with iron proving
algorithms, becomes hungry for more
knowledge. And is even, convinced that the
existence of a higher power or technology
that could exist. That spirited or so called
ghosting, does exist.

Even knowing that other planets have
sustained life for humankind. That, that

Higher Power may exist, because of the plan
to be, is coming to be.

But having, and knowing possessing a
power that could kill millions or billions
with forces only understood to make a deadly
weapon of mass destruction. These words,
become sharper than two-edged swords. But
morally knowing that killing is wrong. Makes
the manifestation to be possible. The laws
of the universe, a super power or a vastly
superiority, to that of humans. But,
intertwined with an invisible force, that
makes magnetism, the dedicated invisible
force or thoughts that make you move, or
come forth. You are meant to be here, right
now. Do not get interrupted.

CHAPTER TWO

Moonbase 33

Moon base 33

The Lost Souls of

The End

The year is December 2666.

Michael is introduced:

"Good Evening, this is Michael
Angelo on VXO-xoxiO..O news at 12:00.

Grab your emergency supplies, get
your families, hurry up, and hide from the
liquid raindrops of Hell, if you can.

Today we are sadly reporting the end
of the world appears to be finally
occurring, and now the end has been bestowed

upon the planet. As many stories of history, and prophecies have warned us in the past to prepare, and pray for this day to never occur. Nothing physically or mentally can really prepare us or yourself for this day. As harsh as that may sound. The fact of the matter is the end has been bestowed upon us all."

Michael turns his head with a smirk on his face, and says;

"Well most of us at least.

33 Crystal Skulls
& The Anti+Christ

BOOK 1 OF 7

www.ingramcontent.com/pod-product-compliance
Lightning Source LLC
Chambersburg PA
CBHW020659030726
47498CB00002B/581